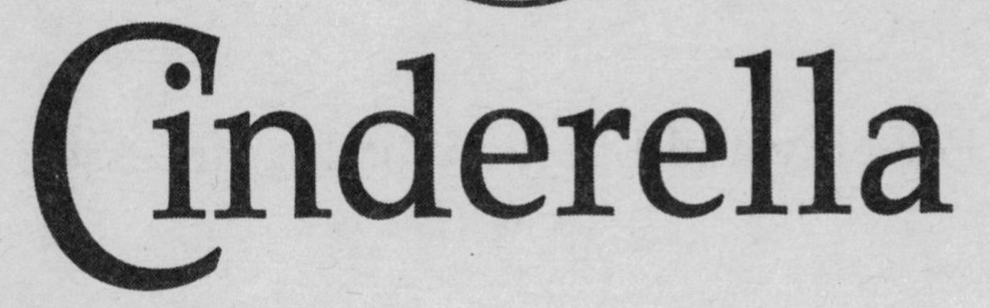

The Junior Novelization

For Lilly and Lucy, my little princesses
—M.L.

 Published in the United States by Random House Children's Books, a division of Random House, Inc., 1745 Broadway, New York, NY 10019, and in Canada by Random House of Canada Limited, Toronto, in conjunction with Disney Enterprises, Inc. Random House and the colophon are registered trademarks of Random House, Inc.

ISBN: 978-0-7364-3007-4

randomhouse.com/kids

Printed in the United States of America

10 9 8 7 6 5 4 3 2 1

Cinderella

The Junior Novelization

Adapted by
Melissa Lagonegro

Chapter 1

Once upon a time in a faraway land, a majestic castle sat high atop a hill overlooking its kingdom. Though the kingdom was small, it flourished, and abounded in strong traditions and peaceful people.

Deep within the kingdom, a grand chateau was home to a widowed man and his beautiful young daughter, Cinderella. Her golden hair and sparkling blue eyes made her lovely to behold, but Cinderella's beauty also came from within. Her kind heart and gentle nature were evident to everyone who met her. She loved her father dearly and enjoyed being with him. She especially loved spending time in the courtyard with her father, her horse, Major, and her puppy, Bruno.

Cinderella's father was equally kind and extremely devoted to his daughter. He loved her greatly and provided her with a luxurious life, but he felt she needed a mother figure. He selected Lady Tremaine as his new wife. She came from a good family and had two daughters, Anastasia and Drizella, both of whom were close to Cinderella's age.

Unfortunately, shortly after the marriage, Cinderella's beloved father died. Cinderella was heartbroken, and she quickly discovered her stepmother's true character. Lady Tremaine was a cold, spiteful, horrid woman who wanted the best only for her own daughters, not for Cinderella. She was deeply jealous of Cinderella's beauty and charm—and she was concerned that Cinderella would easily outshine Anastasia and Drizella. Lady Tremaine would stop at nothing to make Cinderella's life miserable.

Over time, the once stately chateau became run-down and neglected. The sunlit, flower-filled courtyard Cinderella and her father used to enjoy turned dark and dreary. Lady Tremaine spent the family fortune on her two selfish daughters. While

Anastasia and Drizella were pampered and dressed in the finest gowns, Cinderella wore rags. She was humiliated and mistreated. Cinderella was banished from her cozy bedroom to a secluded tower in the chateau and finally was made a servant in her own home. Despite her hardships, she remained kind and gentle.

Cinderella believed happiness would come to her once again. . . .

Chapter 2

Early one morning, but not too early for the birds to start their day, sunshine poured into Cinderella's room as some birds opened her window. A view of the sun-drenched castle in the distance was clear and bright. The sleepy young lady lying nestled in her bed tried to ignore the chirping of her little friends. Dressed in tiny shoes and head scarves, the birds tweeted "Wake up!" into Cinderella's ear. Clutching her pillow, Cinderella sighed and rolled over, pretending to go back to sleep. Unbeknownst to one of the birds, however, Cinderella sneaked her hand from under the covers. She tapped the tip of his tail. The bird was quite surprised. He squeaked and plopped onto the foot of the bed, embarrassed.

His friend laughed, and Cinderella giggled. She was awake after all!

"Well, serves you right, spoiling people's best dreams," Cinderella said playfully to the bird.

The birds continued to chirp and beckon Cinderella toward the window.

"Yes, I know it's a lovely morning, but it was a lovely dream, too," answered Cinderella as she leaned back against her pillow. She always had such wonderful and happy dreams. She hoped that one day those dreams would come true.

The birds chirped.

"What kind of dream?" Cinderella considered their question. "If you tell a wish, it won't come true," she replied. "And after all, a dream is a wish your heart makes."

The birds were satisfied with her answer and sat quietly to listen to her sing a sweet song as she brushed her hair. Cinderella's gentle voice attracted even more birds to the window, and soon she had quite an audience.

The mice that lived between the walls of the chateau awoke and crept through cracks to claim their spots on the bedposts. Jaq, one of Cinderella's dearest mouse friends, sat on top of the post closest to Cinderella. He slowly batted his eyes and smiled as he listened to Cinderella sing.

Ding, dong! Ding, dong! Ding, dong! Cinderella's leisurely wake-up was quickly spoiled when the clock on the palace tower sounded. She grabbed her pillow and pretended to threaten the clock with it. Then she slipped on her shoes and turned toward the window. "I hear you. 'Come on, get up,' you say!" She sighed as the clock struck again. "Time to start another day."

Cinderella tossed her pillow on her bed and threw her frayed brown bedcover in the air. The birds grabbed the corners of the cover and tucked them into place. Four other birds straightened out the wrinkles and plumped her pillow.

Cinderella grabbed her towel and headed across the dull wooden floors to the washbasin in her plain and simple room. A girl mouse wearing a head scarf and dress shooed the male mice out of the room so Cinderella could get ready. Some of the girl mice filled the washbasin with water while some birds dampened the sponge. Others folded her hair ribbon, polished her slippers, and fluffed her dress. They worked busily to help Cinderella get ready for the day ahead.

Chapter 3

Jaq and another mouse scurried under the door into Cinderella's room just as Cinderella finished tying her hair ribbon. They climbed on top of her dresser and babbled in unison.

"Wait a minute, one at a time, please!" said Cinderella as she tried to calm the mice. "Now, Jaq, what's all the fuss about?"

"There's a new mouse in-a the house," Jaq began in his not-quite-perfect mouse chatter. *"Tizavor!"*

"Oh, a *visitor,*" said Cinderella. She clearly understood Jaq's funny speech. Cinderella opened one of her dresser drawers, which was filled with little mice clothes, and pulled out a shirt, a hat, and shoes.

"Please get 'im out!" continued Jaq frantically, seeing that his human friend did not fully understand the situation. "Trap! It's a trap!"

"Well, why didn't you say so?" Cinderella said, springing into action. She grabbed the mouse clothes and went running out of her room, down the long tower staircase. The mice raced after her.

Cinderella found the trap at the bottom of the stairs. She kneeled down and looked in to find a frightened mouse.

"Oh, the poor little thing is scared to death!" She opened the trap. "Jaq, maybe you'd better explain things to him." She gently placed the open trap on the floor. Jaq approached the mouse, who put up his fists, ready to defend himself.

"Now, now, now," Jaq began. "There's nothing to worry about." He pointed to his friends reassuringly. The frightened mouse looked up and saw a group of mice smiling down at him. "We like-a you," continued Jaq. Cinderella looked inside the trap and smiled, too. "Cinderelly really likes-a you, too. She's-a nice." Jaq put his arm around the new mouse's shoulder and led him out of the trap.

Cinderella held up the tiny shirt and shoes she had brought for their new guest. The mouse was rather plump, and Cinderella wasn't sure the clothes would fit. "Let's just slip it on for size," she said, pulling the shirt over his head. "It's a little snug, but it will have to do." After putting on his hat and shoes, it was time for Cinderella to give him a name. "Octavius. But for short, we'll call you Gus."

Jaq turned to Gus the newcomer and nodded in approval. Gus agreed that the name was a good fit. He was excited about his new friends, his new clothes, *and* his new name. He had a feeling that the other mice and Cinderella would take good care of him.

Chapter 4

Cinderella hurried off to start her daily chores. She entered the elegant hallway leading to the rooms where her stepmother and stepsisters slept. The carpet was plush and purple, and the chandelier, ornate and grand, twinkled from the high ceiling. Cinderella opened the velvet curtains of a huge window and the hall was flooded with light.

Cinderella tiptoed toward her stepmother's bedroom door. First on her to-do list was to feed her stepmother's nasty cat, Lucifer. Sneaky and mean, Lucifer loved to stir up trouble but hated to be stirred himself. The overfed cat slept curled in a ball on his own soft, frilly bed in Lady Tremaine's room. Cinderella opened her stepmother's door and politely summoned Lucifer for breakfast. With a stretch and a yawn, Lucifer stood up, turned away from Cinderella, and sat back down. He did not want to be disturbed.

"Lucifer, come here!" Cinderella said in a loud whisper. She wanted the cat to obey her but did not want to wake her sleeping stepmother. Lucifer was startled and jumped up. Since his cozy slumber was officially over and there was food to be had, he gave in and unhurriedly made his way out of the room with his head held high.

"I'm sorry if Your Highness objects to an early breakfast," said Cinderella to Lucifer as he slowly strutted behind her. "It's certainly not my idea to feed you first. It's orders."

Meanwhile, Jaq and Gus stood close to the wall, watching Lucifer follow Cinderella down the stairs. Jaq tried to warn Gus about the mean old cat. But Lucifer didn't intimidate the newcomer at all. Gus laughed and put up his little fists, then stuck out his chest and made to march toward the fat cat. Jaq pulled Gus's tail and dragged him back to the wall. He tried to talk some sense into his new friend.

"Lucifer is not-a funny," he said to Gus. "Lucifer is *mean.*"

Cinderella and Lucifer made their way to the kitchen. Bruno the dog was growling and running in his sleep on a rug by the stove. Cinderella woke her old dog.

"Dreaming again?" she asked as she started to boil water for tea. "Chasing Lucifer?"

Bruno smiled. He and Lucifer did not get along at all. The smug cat was always trying to gain the upper hand.

"You'd better get rid of those dreams," Cinderella said to Bruno. She knew that if Bruno made too much noise and fought with Lucifer, her stepmother would throw him out of the house. "Just learn to like cats," she suggested, making Bruno groan.

As Cinderella placed cups and saucers on a tray, she tried to think positively of the cat. "There must be *something* good about him," she said to Bruno, shrugging. Lucifer scowled at Cinderella. Bruno was quite amused. But Lucifer would have the last laugh. He slyly looked at Cinderella as she started to pour his milk. He slid under Bruno on the rug and scratched him. Bruno reacted angrily and growled. But the sly cat lay on his back and meowed at Cinderella as if he were the victim.

Cinderella stopped pouring the milk and went to intervene. She opened the door and let a defeated Bruno out of the house. "I know it isn't easy, but we should all at least try to get along together," she said to him. Cinderella put the dish of milk down in front of Lucifer. "That includes you, Your Majesty," she added.

Lucifer swirled his milk with his paw. With a hateful look, he watched Cinderella head off to attend to her other morning chores.

Chapter 5

Not only did Cinderella have to take care of things inside the house, but she had chores to do outside as well. Each morning she fed the animals in the barnyard.

"Come on, everybody, breakfast!" she called. The chickens, ducks, and geese waddled over for their food. Cinderella knew the animals appreciated her, and she enjoyed being in their company out in the warm sunshine.

The mice enjoyed the morning feeding even more. Jaq led four mice through the walls and down to a hole into the kitchen. They were headed outside to eat, too—but they had to be careful.

"Lucifer!" Jaq warned the other mice. "How

are we gonna get out?" Lucifer blocked their path to the outside door. He was still stirring his milk. The mice needed a plan.

Jaq had an idea. One of the mice would creep out and get Lucifer to chase him away from the door. The other mice would sneak by, run outside, and gather food for breakfast. The mice agreed it was a great plan.

Instead of drawing straws, they drew their tails to decide who would confront Lucifer. They stood in a circle and turned their backs to each other, intertwining their tails. Jaq pulled one tail from the group and held on to it as the mice all hopped out of the circle. He ended up holding his own tail! He would be the one to play the game of cat-and-mouse. Gus proudly shook Jaq's hand, wishing him well.

Jaq was nervous as he made his way toward the cat. He sneaked up to Lucifer and crawled under his arm. With one swift kick, he startled Lucifer, whose face ended up in his bowl of milk.

With that, the chase ensued, and everything went according to plan. Lucifer drove Jaq into a corner where there were two small mouse holes.

Jaq jumped into one hole and Lucifer clawed at it, trying to snatch his quick-footed foe. Jaq popped his head out of the other hole and waved his hat. He signaled to the other mice that they were free to start their escape.

The four mice scooted through the kitchen and out the door, with Gus pulling up the rear. Outside, they watched the chickens peck for food and Major, the horse, eat out of Cinderella's palm. Then they jumped up and waved their hands, letting Cinderella know they were there, too.

"Oh, there you are," she said to the mice. "I was wondering." She stuck her hand into her apron and pulled out a big handful of corn kernels. "Breakfast is served," she said, tossing the corn to the mice. Excitedly, three of the mice quickly picked up pieces. But Gus, the newcomer, was a little too slow. After he fought the chickens for his food, Cinderella saw him standing there empty-handed and shooed the chickens away. Then she gave Gus his own big pile of corn.

Back in the kitchen, Jaq kept Lucifer occupied at the mouse holes and away from the door. He waved to his friends, signaling for them to return inside. Three mice hurried through the kitchen, but one dropped a kernel of corn. Even though Gus could hardly carry his own kernels, he stopped to pick up the dropped piece. He tried to carry all the corn, but it fell out of his hands.

Lucifer heard the sound of the scattering kernels. He quickly turned toward Gus. Jaq panicked and tried to distract Lucifer again by pulling on the cat's whisker. Lucifer was not a bit fazed. He had his eye on the plump mouse. Gus was unaware of the danger as he tried to pick up his food.

Still trying to stop Lucifer, Jaq pulled on the cat's tail but only ended up with a face full of cat hair.

Lucifer made his way over to Gus, who finally had a good grasp on the corn. Unfortunately, he couldn't see where he was going because the pile of food in his arms was so high. He walked right up to Lucifer's mouth! When he realized where he was, Gus dropped the food and ran as fast as he could, but Lucifer had grabbed his tail. The poor mouse was just running in place! Thinking quickly, Jaq pushed a broom, which landed right on Lucifer's head—*thump!* Jaq sighed with relief as Gus escaped from Lucifer's grasp.

Gus wasn't free for long. Lucifer spotted him climbing up the tablecloth and onto the table. Gus thought he was in the clear. He sat on a saucer and tried to catch his breath. Lucifer sneaked up behind him and slammed a teacup upside down on the saucer. Gus was trapped!

Just then, the call bell rang.

Chapter 6

"All right, all right!" Cinderella replied. She ran into the kitchen from outside. She hung her head scarf beside the door and took off her shoes. "I'm coming!"

Anastasia and Drizella were summoning Cinderella. They were awake and ready for their breakfast.

Lucifer ducked under the tablecloth when Cinderella came inside. He waited for just the right moment to grab Gus.

The bell rang again and again. "Cinderella!" the two stepsisters yelled.

Cinderella quickly went to the table and set more teacups upside down on their saucers. Then she ran to the stove to get the teakettle.

Lucifer went back to the table to search for Gus. But he was confused to see three upside-down teacups. He didn't remember which cup Gus was under.

"Cinderella!" called Anastasia. The bell rang again.

Cinderella poured hot water into the last of three teapots. On each of three trays she placed a teapot, a cup and saucer, and a bowl of oatmeal. Balancing the trays carefully, she carried them out of the kitchen.

Lucifer had lost his chance—Gus had escaped on one of the trays. Cinderella had no idea she was carrying the escapee.

With a tray in each hand and one on her head, Cinderella swiftly made it up the stairs. Lucifer stayed close behind, trying to catch a glimpse of Gus.

Cinderella walked into Drizella's room. "Good morning, Drizella. Sleep well?" she asked.

"Take that ironing and have it back in an hour!" yelled Drizella.

"Yes, Drizella," replied Cinderella. She left the

room with one less tray, but she now had a basket of clothes to be ironed.

"Good morning, Anastasia," Cinderella said, making her way into her other stepsister's room.

"Well, it's about time," replied Anastasia snootily. "Don't forget the mending, and don't be all day getting it done, either!"

"Yes, Anastasia," said Cinderella, leaving with another pile of clothes. She headed into her stepmother's room with one last tray.

"Good morning, Stepmother," she said.

"Pick up the laundry and get on with your duties," said Lady Tremaine.

"Yes, Stepmother," replied Cinderella, leaving the room. In one hand she carried a large basket of Drizella's clothes. In the other hand she carried a box of Anastasia's clothes. And on her head she carried a bundle of Lady Tremaine's laundry. She started down the stairs.

Meanwhile, Lucifer had followed Cinderella to every room. He was still looking for Gus. Then it happened. It was exactly what Lucifer was waiting for . . . the mouse had been discovered!

"Ahhhhhhh!" screamed Anastasia. Gus ran

through her room and slipped under the door. Lucifer was waiting there to catch him.

Cinderella ran back up the stairs. Anastasia charged out of her room. "You did it! You did it on purpose!" she yelled, waving her finger in Cinderella's face. "Mother!" Anastasia ran into her mother's room.

Drizella came out to see what all the commotion was about. "Now what did you do?" she asked Cinderella. Then she followed her sister into their mother's room.

"She put it there . . . a big ugly mouse under my teacup," Drizella told her mother. Cinderella was shocked when she heard. She looked accusingly down at Lucifer.

"All right, Lucifer," she said. "What did you do with him?"

Lucifer shrugged and played dumb. But Cinderella wasn't a fool. She picked Lucifer up by his neck. Gus lay curled in a ball underneath Lucifer's foot.

"Oh, poor little Gus," she said. Gus took advantage of his freedom and scurried away into a hole in the wall.

Just then, Lady Tremaine called for Cinderella. Cinderella walked to the room with Lucifer happily slinking around her feet. He knew Cinderella was going to get in big trouble. The stepsisters stood outside the door and looked at Cinderella with evil grins. They also knew she was going to pay for what had happened.

Cinderella entered the room and closed the door behind her. The room was dark and cold, just like the woman who slept in it. Cinderella stood awaiting her fate as evil eyes glared at her.

"Now, it seems we have time on our hands," began Lady Tremaine. Cinderella tried to explain but was quickly shushed by her stepmother. "Time for vicious practical jokes," Lady Tremaine continued. "Perhaps we could put that time to better use."

She began to give Cinderella a long list of additional chores. She even ordered Cinderella to give Lucifer a bath.

Cinderella and Lucifer sighed. Neither of them was looking forward to that.

Chapter 7

Not too far away, the royal palace grounds seemed peaceful and calm. White doves flocked to a window ledge singing a sweet song. But they were quickly disrupted when a crown came crashing through the window!

Inside the palace, things were not so peaceful and calm. Broken statues and vases were scattered across the dark hardwood floors. The King was mad, and he wasn't holding back his anger. He was short and plump, with a long white mustache that curled up on the ends. He also had quite a temper. He was loud, demanding, and over-the-top, yet he was also a bit of a softy. He longed for the day when the sound of children's laughter would fill the castle. He wanted grandchildren and he wanted them immediately. The only way for that to happen was for his son, the Prince, to find a bride and get married.

"My son has been avoiding his responsibilities long enough!" he yelled, banging his fist on a long marble desk. "It's high time he married and settled down!"

"Of course, Your Majesty," responded the Grand Duke, peering out from behind a large shield hanging on the wall. He was trying to avoid being hit by flying objects. He was the King's most trusted advisor, and even though he supported the King in every way, he felt marriage was sacred and shouldn't be forced upon anyone—not even the Prince. "But we must be patient!"

"I am patient!" hollered the King. Quickly his demeanor changed. He sank into his big chair and became melancholy. "I'm not getting any younger, you know. I want to see my grandchildren before I turn over the kingdom to the Prince."

"I understand, sire," the Duke replied quickly—and solicitously.

The King walked the Duke around the enormous room. He pointed to the gigantic pictures on the walls. They were like a shrine to his beloved son. One picture was of the Prince as a happy baby, sitting on the King's lap. Another was of the King giving a toddler Prince a piggyback ride. The third picture was of an older Prince riding his horse, with his father in the distance. The last picture was the biggest. It was a huge portrait of the Prince on his majestic white horse—but without his father. The Prince was grown now, and the King was proud of him—but he also missed the days when the Prince had still been his little boy.

"I'm lonely in this desolate palace," the King said, whimpering. "I want to hear the pitter-patter of little feet again." He rested his head on the Grand Duke's chest and sobbed.

"Now, now, Your Majesty." The Grand Duke began patting the King's head. "Perhaps if we just left him alone . . ."

"Left him alone!" the King bellowed.

The Duke went flying behind a desk. From this safe position, he tried to explain that it was best not to interfere when it came to matters of the heart. But the King wouldn't listen. The Prince would soon return from a long trip, and the King had an idea.

"What could be more natural than a ball to celebrate his return?" asked the King. "And if all the eligible maidens in my kingdom just happen to be there, why, he is bound to show interest in one of them, isn't he?"

The Duke was scared, and quivered in his chair as he listened to the King rant. The King grabbed the Duke by his shirt and demanded an answer. "ISN'T HE?" he asked again.

"Ye-ye-ye-yes, sire," responded the Duke, trembling.

Then the King smiled as he described the perfect ball. Romantic lighting and music would set the tone for a beautiful evening that was bound to make his son fall in love! He chuckled with delight.

"It can't possibly fail!" he declared.

The Duke wanted to please the King. "Very well, sire, I will arrange the ball for—"

"Tonight!" the King ordered.

"Tonight?" repeated the Duke.

"Tonight!" shouted the King in the Duke's face. "And see that every eligible maid is there! Understand?"

"Yes, Your Majesty," said the Duke, defeated, as the King walked away.

Chapter 8

Back at the chateau, Drizella and Anastasia were in the middle of their music lesson. They wore fancy dresses and had giant bows in their hair. Though they were neat and primped, they were awkward and obnoxious. Drizella sang while Anastasia played the flute. Both girls were completely off-key. Lady Tremaine happily accompanied her tone-deaf daughters on a large black grand piano.

All through the lesson, the girls tried to outdo each other. With every note, Drizella sang louder and more off-key as Anastasia blew harder into her flute.

Lucifer sat on a velvet bench in the same room. He was so pained by the horrific noise that he covered his ears with his paws. Still miserable, he tried hiding under a big, fluffy red pillow. Finally, he couldn't take the noise any longer. He jumped off the bench and ran out, slamming the door behind him. He shook his head and tried to recover. Then he walked toward the stairs and heard someone singing the same song the sisters were singing . . . but who could it be?

It was Cinderella—and her voice was beautiful. She was at the bottom of the staircase scrubbing the black-and-green marble floors in the grand entrance. She dipped her rag into a bubble-filled washbasin. A giant bubble rose and landed on her finger. She looked at her reflection in the bubble, fluffed her hair, and continued to sing sweetly as she scrubbed the entire floor.

Instead of enjoying the sound of Cinderella's lovely voice, Lucifer saw an opportunity to wreak havoc. He spotted a huge pile of dirt in a dustpan. He then glared at Cinderella.

After stepping in the pile of dirt, Lucifer paraded around on Cinderella's sparkling clean floor. Then he resumed his position on the stairs.

The cat smugly looked up at Cinderella.

Cinderella caught his eye. She saw him surrounded by dirty paw prints.

"Oh, Lucifer!" she cried. Then she turned around and saw the filthy floor—the floor she had just scrubbed on her hands and knees. It was covered with paw prints. "You mean old thing!" she yelled. She went after him with her broom. "I'm just going to have to teach you a lesson—"

Suddenly, there was a knock at the door.

"Open in the name of the King!" shouted a man from outside.

Jaq and Gus curiously peeked out of a mouse hole as Cinderella opened the door.

"An urgent message from His Imperial Majesty," said the messenger, handing Cinderella a letter. She thanked him, curtsied politely, and shut the door. The mice ran toward her for a closer look.

"Uh, what's it say?" asked Gus.

"I don't know," replied Cinderella. She examined the letter, then looked upstairs as the music started again. "He says it's urgent."

Cinderella and the mice winced as they heard

Anastasia and Drizella hit an exceptionally bad note. "Maybe I should interrupt the . . . 'music lesson'?" she said, giggling. The mice giggled, too, and watched Cinderella head up the stairs.

Meanwhile, Drizella continued to get every note wrong. Anastasia played her flute and got her finger stuck in one of the holes. She tried to wiggle it out while still playing and ended up hitting Drizella under her chin. Drizella was furious. She grabbed the flute and hit Anastasia over the head with it. Anastasia hit her back, and a fight ensued.

"Girls, girls!" Lady Tremaine admonished. She stopped playing the piano and waved a finger at her daughters. "Remember, above all . . . self-control."

Cinderella knocked on the door and entered the grand room. Lady Tremaine was furious. She stood up from her piano bench. Her dress was formal and she was wearing a big green brooch, but her evil eyes were her most noticeable accessory.

"Cinderella, I warned you never to interrupt our—" she began testily.

"But this just arrived from the palace," interjected Cinderella, holding up the letter.

"From the palace?" screamed the stepsisters. They ran to Cinderella, snatched the envelope from her hand, and ripped it open. But Lady Tremaine calmly took it from them. Her eyes lit up as she began to read the letter out loud. There was going to be a ball in honor of the Prince, and every eligible maiden in the kingdom was required to attend.

"A ball!" cheered the stepsisters. They squirmed with excitement and batted their eyelashes.

Cinderella was equally excited. "Why, that means I can go, too!" she exclaimed. Anastasia and Drizella laughed. There they stood in their fine gowns while Cinderella wore dirty and tattered clothes, holding a broom in her hand. They mocked Cinderella for her ridiculous idea, but Cinderella held her head high. She stood proudly and walked deeper into the room to confront the ladies.

"I'm still a member of the family," she said, trying to assert herself.

Gus and Jaq had been watching through a mouse hole the whole time. They were proud of Cinderella for standing up for herself.

Lady Tremaine hadn't been expecting her stepdaughter's bold statement. The wheels in her scheming brain turned as she thought of a response. She had a plan.

"Well, I see no reason why you can't go . . . ," began Lady Tremaine. The stepsisters were shocked. "If you get all your work done."

"Oh, I will . . . I promise!" said Cinderella joyously.

"And if you can find something suitable to wear," finished Lady Tremaine.

"I'm sure I can!" replied Cinderella. "Oh, thank you, Stepmother!" She ran out of the room, closing the door behind her. Gus and Jaq followed.

Drizella and Anastasia rushed to their mother. They were angry and confused. Why on earth would she let Cinderella go to the ball?

"Mother, do you realize what you just said?" asked Drizella.

"Of course," said Lady Tremaine with a sinister smile. "I said *if*."

"Oh!" replied Drizella, nodding. "IF!"

Lady Tremaine, Anastasia, and Drizella all cackled. They were about to make Cinderella's life more miserable than ever.

Chapter 9

Cinderella could hardly contain herself. She rushed back to her room in search of something to wear to the ball. She opened a big old trunk. The trunk was dusty, but the items in it were dear to her. She pulled out a pink-and-white dress. It had puffy pink sleeves with white ruffled edges. The bottom of the dress was white, with more ruffled edges. Cinderella twirled around the room holding it up to her chest. Four girl mice sat on the top of the trunk watching her spin as two little birds flapped their wings with joy.

"Isn't it lovely?" Cinderella asked her friends. "It was my mother's."

"It's old!" said Suzy the mouse.

With the help of the two birds, Cinderella lifted the dress onto a dressmaker's dummy she had in her room. "Well, maybe it is a little old-fashioned, but I'll fix that," she replied. She fluffed the dress as Gus and Jaq entered the room. A sewing book was in her workbasket. Cinderella kneeled down and flipped through the pages. She was determined to find something in there for inspiration. The mice and birds surrounded her, brimming with anticipation.

"Uh-huh, this one!" she said, leaning the open book up against the trunk. The mice came in for a closer look and agreed that the dress she had chosen was lovely. Cinderella examined the dress in the book. She would have to shorten the sleeves of her mother's dress, add a sash and a ruffle, and get something for the collar. It would take time, but it was doable—and the final product would be a beautiful and elegant dress, perfect for a royal ball.

Cinderella's dressmaking plans were quickly cut short.

"Cinderella!" yelled one stepsister.

"Oh, now what do they want?" said Cinderella, frustrated.

"Cinderella!" called the other stepsister and Lady Tremaine.

Over and over, they called her name.

Poor Cinderella stood up and walked over to her dress on the dummy. "Oh, well, guess my dress will just have to wait," she said sadly. All three voices called for Cinderella again and again. "All right, all right, I'm coming!" she replied. With a heavy heart, she left her room.

Jaq and Gus followed her to the door.

"Poor Cinderelly," said Jaq. He hated that her stepmother and stepsisters kept her so busy. He looked up at her dress and knew she would never have time to fix it before the ball. All the mice realized this, and they shook their heads in disappointment.

Suzy looked at the dress and then the sewing book. She had an idea. "We can do it!" she said. The mice jumped for joy. They could fix the dress—it was a great idea! Birds flew into the room and offered their help as well. They all quickly got to work. They grabbed spools of thread, scissors, a needle, and a tape measure.

While the birds and the other mice started on the dress, Jaq and Gus set out to find some special trimmings. They ran through the walls of the chateau, sliding down wooden planks and swinging across spiderwebs. They popped their heads through a wall where they heard lots of activity. Anastasia and Drizella were throwing clothes at Cinderella. They ordered her to mend, iron, and sew everything in the pile. The pile was so big Cinderella could hardly hold it.

Lady Tremaine entered with her own demands. "When you're through and before you begin your regular chores," she began, "I have a few little things."

"Very well," replied Cinderella obediently. She left the room with the huge pile of clothes.

Lady Tremaine's wicked plan had been set in motion. She knew there was no way Cinderella could fulfill all their demands and still have time to find something to wear.

Meanwhile, Anastasia and Drizella were still yelling and screaming. The spoiled girls complained that their clothes and accessories were just not good enough.

"This sash—well, I wouldn't be seen dead in it!" Anastasia yelled, throwing a gorgeous pink sash to the ground.

"These beads . . . I'm sick of looking at them. TRASH!" declared Drizella, throwing a lovely blue beaded necklace on the floor.

They huffed and stormed out of the room, slamming the door behind them.

Jaq and Gus were thrilled! The sash and necklace would make Cinderella's dress perfect. The trimmings they were looking for were only a few steps away. But those steps would not be easy. Lucifer was asleep right in their path. They tiptoed under the footstool holding the snoozing cat. They grabbed the long pink sash and ran back under the footstool, but Lucifer woke up. Luckily, the mice were too quick, and they pulled the long sash down into the mouse hole, infuriating the cat. Gus and Jaq popped through another hole. This time they had their eyes on the necklace. But Lucifer ran over and sat on it.

Jaq whispered into Gus's ear and they cooked up one of their sneaky plans. Jaq jumped out of the mouse hole and tiptoed across the floor. He sneaked past Lucifer and walked right into a pile of the stepsisters' clothes. He hummed a tune and plucked buttons off a shirt, trying to get Lucifer's attention. His plan was to distract Lucifer so Gus could grab the beads.

Lucifer was about to pounce on Jaq. Then he realized that he was no longer sitting on the beads—and Gus was headed straight for them! The sly cat ran back to the beads and sat right on top of them again. This time he slid his body toward Jaq, dragging the necklace along with him. But Jaq continued to tease the cat. Finally, Lucifer couldn't resist the chase any longer, and he jumped into the pile of clothes after Jaq.

Gus grabbed the beads, but he was not very light on his feet. He ran into the wall. The necklace broke and the beads scattered. Lucifer stopped chasing Jaq and turned his attention to Gus.

Luckily, Lucifer got stuck in the sleeve of one of the dresses. The tight squeeze slowed the cat down and enabled Jaq to help Gus gather all the beads one by one and escape through the mouse hole.

Once again, Lucifer was left empty-handed.

Back in Cinderella's room, the girl mice were sewing while the birds measured and laid pieces of fabric into place. Gus and Jaq returned with the sash and the beads. The sash was used to make a beautiful bow at the top of the dress. The rest of the sash wrapped around to the bottom of the dress. The beads were restrung to make the perfect necklace. The mice and birds were the ideal dressmaking team. The once old-fashioned dress looked new and elegant. Cinderella was going to love it!

Chapter 10

It was eight o' clock in the evening, and guests were beginning to arrive at the palace for the ball. Coaches waited in line at the palace entrance, dropping off young women who were hoping to win the Prince's heart.

At the chateau, Cinderella looked out the window and saw a coachman and carriage waiting. While her stepmother and stepsisters primped for the big event, she had been doing dozens of chores. She had finally finished everything, but she hadn't had time to fix her dress. Cinderella was tired and disappointed. With her broom in her hand and her head hanging low, Cinderella sadly walked to her stepmother's room. She knocked on the door and Lady Tremaine opened it.

"The carriage is here," said Cinderella solemnly. She turned around and walked away.

"Why, Cinderella," began her stepmother, feigning concern. "You're not ready, child."

"I'm not going," Cinderella answered.

"Not going," echoed Lady Tremaine. "What a shame." She smiled at Anastasia and Drizella, who were peering from behind the door. They all got a good laugh out of Cinderella's unhappiness. Lady Tremaine's plan had worked.

Cinderella walked back up to her dark room and leaned on the windowsill. She stared dreamily out the window and imagined what it would be like at the royal ball. The palace glowed in the distance, lighting up the night sky. It was a wondrous sight—but Cinderella would only see it from afar.

Suddenly, her room filled with light. She turned around and saw the birds opening her armoire. A glowing candle revealed a dress—the perfect dress—the one *she* had not had the time to make!

"Surprise!" cheered the mice.

Cinderella grabbed the dress and held it up. She twirled around the room with joy.

"Oh, thank you so much!" she said.

Meanwhile, Lady Tremaine, Anastasia, and Drizella were walking down the stairs in their finest gowns. They headed to the front door but were suddenly stopped.

"Wait, please wait for me!" called Cinderella. She floated down the stairs in her new gown. It fit her perfectly, and she beamed with happiness.

Her stepmother and stepsisters gasped. They were not expecting to see Cinderella, let alone see her look so perfectly beautiful.

"Think it will do?" asked Cinderella, twirling around to show off her dress. The mice were watching from the balcony and were thrilled to see the stepfamily on the spot. Anastasia and Drizella were furious, and looked to their mother to do something immediately. They would not have Cinderella go to the ball with them!

The deceitful Lady Tremaine motioned for her daughters to control themselves. Her scheming mind was at work, and once again she had plan.

"After all, we did make a bargain . . . didn't we?" she said to her daughters.

Cinderella smiled. The stepsisters were shocked. Lady Tremaine walked toward Cinderella. "And I never go back on my word," she continued.

Jaq looked on suspiciously. He knew Lady Tremaine had something up her sleeve.

Lady Tremaine got even closer to Cinderella, who became a bit uncomfortable. Lady Tremaine lifted up the beaded necklace Cinderella was wearing—the beaded necklace that had belonged to Drizella. "How very clever . . . these beads, they give it just the right touch," she said, turning toward Drizella. "Don't you think so, Drizella?"

"Why, you little thief!" screamed Drizella, understanding her mother's hint perfectly. "They're *my* beads!" She stormed toward Cinderella and ripped the necklace from her neck. "Give them here!"

"Look, that's my sash!" yelled Anastasia. She tore the sash right off the dress. The stepsisters ripped Cinderella's dress while calling her names.

"Oh, stop, please!" cried Cinderella. She covered her face and was spun around like a top as her stepsisters pulled at every inch of her dress.

"Girls!" said Lady Tremaine. She opened the front door and beckoned her daughters. "That's quite enough. Hurry along." The stepsisters walked proudly out the door with Lady Tremaine close behind. "I won't have you upsetting yourselves," she continued. She followed them to the carriage, leaving Cinderella stranded and devastated in the hallway.

Lady Tremaine and her daughters had not only ruined Cinderella's dress, they had also tried to ruin her spirit—and that made them very proud of themselves.

Chapter 11

Cinderella was heartbroken. Crying, she ran through the dark halls of the house and out into the garden. Bruno and Major were in the stable and watched Cinderella race past them in tears.

The garden was dark and run-down. It looked just like Cinderella felt. She ran to a bench, kneeled beside it, and laid her head down on the bench and sobbed. Bruno and Major walked out of the stable in hopes of comforting poor Cinderella. They hung their heads in sadness. Gus, Jaq, and two other mice watched Cinderella from an outside step. They were heartbroken, too.

"It's just no use," said Cinderella, sobbing. "There's nothing left to believe in . . . nothing."

Suddenly, sparkles of white light flashed in the garden. The animals watched as the twinkling lights got brighter and surrounded Cinderella. The sparkles came together—and turned into a woman! The woman sat on the bench with Cinderella's head in her lap. Short and a bit plump, she had white hair, and she wore a blue dress and hooded cloak. A dark pink scarf tied in a big bow was wrapped around her neck. Her smile was reassuring.

"Nothing, my dear?" said the woman, stroking Cinderella's head. "Now, you don't really mean that."

"Oh, but I do!" responded Cinderella, sniffling.

"Nonsense, child!" said the woman. "If you'd lost all your faith, I couldn't be here—and here I am!" She lifted Cinderella's head and looked her in the eyes.

Cinderella gasped.

"Oh, come now, dry those tears," said the woman, helping Cinderella to her feet. "You can't go to the ball looking like that."

"The ball?" asked Cinderella. She looked down at her torn dress. "But I'm not—"

"Of course you are!" said the woman. The

mice smiled at the thought of Cinderella's having another chance to go to the ball. "But we'll have to hurry, because even miracles take a little time." The woman pushed up her sleeves and raised her arms. She was ready to perform a miracle. She looked around. She seemed to be missing something.

"What in the world did I do with that magic wand?" she asked, searching inside her big sleeves.

"Magic wand?" asked Cinderella curiously. Suddenly, Cinderella put everything together and a huge smile came across her face. "Why, then you must be—"

"Your fairy godmother," interrupted the woman. "Of course!" She continued to look for her wand, checking under the bench. After shaking out her dress one last time, she remembered that she had simply put it away. With a twirl of her finger, the wand magically appeared in her hand. Cinderella's jaw dropped and her eyes opened wide. Even the mice were shocked.

The Fairy Godmother looked Cinderella over. Deep in thought, she pointed her wand at the girl. She waved the wand up and down. Little bursts of sparkles came from it. "I'd say the first thing you need is . . . a pumpkin," she said.

"A pumpkin?" asked Cinderella, holding her tattered dress. She thought a new dress was surely the first thing she needed.

The Fairy Godmother spotted a large pumpkin with its vines still rooted in the ground. She struggled for a moment to remember her magic words, but they finally came to her. She raised her arms and waved her wand.

"Bibbidi-bobbidi-boo!" she exclaimed.

Sparkling lights made a trail from the wand to the giant pumpkin. Suddenly, the pumpkin and its vines rose from the ground and bounced over to Cinderella and her fairy godmother. The animals were in awe and didn't know what to make of the giant dancing pumpkin. The mice ran to hide. Bruno and Major huddled together, trying to avoid the lengthening vines. The pumpkin grew larger and larger. The vines shaped themselves into wheels. The plain old pumpkin turned into a sparkling carriage! The animals ran toward it in amazement.

"Oh, it's beautiful!" raved Cinderella. She came

in for a closer look.

"Yes, isn't it?" agreed the Fairy Godmother. But the elegant coach needed more. With another wave of her wand, she turned the four mice into glorious white horses with tall pink-feathered headpieces and golden harnesses. The horses took their places at the front of the carriage.

The Fairy Godmother waved her wand again—this time at Cinderella's old horse, Major. He turned into a fine coachman! He took his place at the front of the carriage, holding the reins. The horse-turned-coachman admired himself and tipped his hat in appreciation to the Fairy Godmother.

"Well, that does it, I guess . . . ," began the Fairy Godmother. She raised her hand to her chin. She knew there was still something missing. "Oh, yes, the finishing touch, and that's you!"

Cinderella closed her eyes in anticipation. She knew the next round of magic had to be for her. She needed a new dress! But the magic was intended for Bruno, not Cinderella. The Fairy Godmother turned him into a footman for the carriage. Like Major, he admired his new human form, then proudly held the carriage door open for Cinderella.

"Well, well, hop in, my dear. We can hardly waste time," said the Fairy Godmother, beckoning Cinderella toward the carriage.

"But . . . uh," stammered Cinderella. She held her dress, politely trying to indicate that it needed some assistance. "Don't you think my dress—

"Yes, it's lovely, dear," interrupted the Fairy Godmother. She smiled and closed her eyes. But once she opened them again, she was in shock. She finally noticed the state of Cinderella's dress. "Good heavens, child! You can't go in that!"

Cinderella sighed with relief. She then smiled and shook her head in agreement. It was her turn for a little magic, and she could hardly contain her excitement.

The Fairy Godmother approached Cinderella and used the wand to take her measurements. She examined Cinderella's slim physique and alluring eye color. The Fairy Godmother wanted something simple yet elegant, and most of all, new. She stepped back and waved her wand. Spirals of sparkling lights engulfed Cinderella from her feet to the top of her head. As the sparkles cascaded around her, Cinderella was transformed!

The divine ball gown was a lovely shade of blue to match her eyes. The bodice was form-fitting, while the skirt flowed loosely from the waist down. Long white gloves reached just past Cinderella's elbows. A simple necklace and sparkling earrings topped off the look. Her hair was up, and a shimmering headband kept it all in place.

"Oh, it's a beautiful dress!" Cinderella lifted the gown off the floor and twirled toward the carriage. "And look, glass slippers!" she said, pointing to the shoes. She danced over to her fairy godmother. "Why, it's like a dream. A wonderful dream come true!"

"Yes, my child," agreed the Fairy Godmother. She quickly became more serious. "But like all dreams, I'm afraid this can't last forever. You'll have only till midnight, and then—"

"Midnight? Oh, thank you!" interrupted Cinderella. She admired her reflection in the fountain while birds twittered their approval.

But the Fairy Godmother continued with her warning.

"You must understand, my dear: on the stroke of twelve the spell will be broken and everything will be as it was before," she warned.

"Oh, I understand," replied Cinderella. She approached the Fairy Godmother with pure joy and gratitude. "It's more than I ever hoped for." The woman was touched and held Cinderella's face in her hands. But their special moment was quickly cut short when the Fairy Godmother realized the time. It was getting late! She nudged Cinderella toward the carriage and the footman helped her in. Cinderella looked out the window and smiled at her fairy godmother. She waved goodbye as the horses began to gallop away. Delighted, the Fairy Godmother waved back. Then, with a poof, she disappeared into thin air.

The carriage raced up and down hills, over a bridge, and through the streets of the town. The palace was in sight, and Cinderella could hardly wait to arrive.

Chapter 12

The palace was buzzing with young ladies waiting to meet the Prince. Eager maidens were dressed in their finest gowns, and each one hoped for the chance to win the Prince's heart.

The grand ballroom was majestic and massive. The walls were covered with ornate trim and long draperies. Crystal chandeliers hung from the ceiling. Music played by the royal orchestra filled the air.

A long, narrow red carpet stretched across the center of the shiny tiled floor. At one end of the carpet, the ladies of the kingdom were assembled, each patiently waiting for the court announcer to call her name from a long list of attendees. Once called, the young lady would walk down the long red carpet for the opportunity of a lifetime.

At the other end of that carpet stood the very handsome Prince. He was tall, with dark brown hair and eyes. He wore a regal red-and-gold suit and greeted the ladies like a gentleman. As each lady curtsied, he bowed graciously. Though the Prince was smiling politely, his heart was not really in the royal proceedings. He was actually quite bored. This was not the way he wanted to meet the love of his life.

The court announcer continued to call names from his long list and the ball carried on. A huge tapestry of the royal family crest was draped from a large balcony overlooking the dance floor. On that balcony, high above the crowd, the King sat in his large red velvet chair. He watched the reception with the Grand Duke by his side. He was not pleased with his son's lack of enthusiasm.

"The boy isn't cooperating," he said, throwing his hands up in the air. He was frustrated. He just wanted his son to find a wife!

The Grand Duke shrugged and grinned as if

to say "I told you so." He leaned on the King's chair and rolled his monocle up and down like a yo-yo. Having this ball was not a good way to find a bride for the Prince, and the Duke was proud of himself for knowing that.

The King slumped down in his chair and held his head in his hands. He closed his eyes and wrinkled his nose in dissatisfaction. He perked up when the next lady walked toward his son. She was attractive, thought the King. Surely the Prince would agree. He was expecting a warm response from his son, but instead, the Prince yawned, covered his mouth, and peered up at his father.

"I can't understand it!" yelled the King, banging his fist on the balcony's ledge. "There must be at least one who would make a suitable mother!"

The Grand Duke stopped playing with his monocle and shushed the King.

The King covered his mouth and cleared his throat. He realized what he had said. "Suitable *wife*," he said, correcting himself, and once again slumped down into his chair. The King had only one thing on his mind—he wanted the mother of his future grandchild to be chosen from the crowd. With the way the night was going, things didn't look very promising.

And then the young woman in the blue dress walked in.

Chapter 13

A stunning young lady arrived at the palace, wearing a dazzling blue ball gown. She walked up the stairs to the inside hall and stopped. The entranceway was magnificent. She looked around, took a deep breath, and proceeded down the long hallway. Palace guards flanked the entrance. They stood at attention, but they all followed her with their eyes. They simply couldn't help watching the girl.

The young lady slowly walked up another grand staircase carpeted in red velvet. She finally made her way up to the grand ballroom.

Meanwhile, the court announcer continued his introductions.

Cinderella looks out at the royal palace
as she dreams of a different life.

Cinderella is cheerful and kind as she
prepares for another day of chores.

Cinderella's little friends are excited
to help her get ready for the royal ball!

Cinderella's evil stepmother and stepsisters
leave for the ball after making sure Cinderella
is not able to go with them.

Bibbidi-bobbidi-boo! Cinderella's fairy godmother transforms a pumpkin into a fancy carriage.

The Fairy Godmother uses magic to make a dress for Cinderlla—but she warns Cinderella that the spell will be broken at midnight.

Everyone in the kingdom has come
to the ball. The palace is sparkling!

When the Prince sees Cinderella,
it's love at first sight!

The Prince leads Cinderella
onto the dance floor.

The Prince and Cinderella share
a magical moment in each other's arms.

Suddenly, the clock begins to strike midnight! Cinderella was having such a wonderful night that she lost track of time. Now she must go!

Cinderella loses a glass slipper as she hurries from the palace.

The King sends the Grand Duke to find the maiden who lost the glass slipper. That slipper gets broken, but Cinderella has the other one.

The glass slipper fits perfectly on Cinderella's tiny foot!

The Prince marries Cinderella.

Cinderella and the Prince live happily ever after!

“The Mademoiselles Drizella and Anastasia Tremaine,” he proclaimed. The sisters fluffed their dresses and hair, preparing for their big moment. Anastasia turned and kneeled down to adjust her dress. She stepped on Drizella’s dress at the same time and caused Drizella to get mad and stumble slightly. Drizella then pulled her dress from under Anastasia’s feet and almost made her sister fall flat on her face. Drizella started up the carpet without Anastasia, who eventually collected herself and went running after her sister. The girls finally made their way up to the Prince and curtsied.

The Prince couldn’t help noticing how awkward and gawky the two girls were. He immediately knew that the Tremaine sisters were not his type. He sighed and looked up at the ceiling, wishing the evening were over.

The King shuddered at the sight of the sisters. “I give up!” he said, shaking his head as he watched Anastasia and Drizella greet the Prince. “Even I couldn’t expect the boy to—”

But the King was interrupted by the smirking Grand Duke.

"Well, if I may say so, Your Majesty, I did try to warn you, but you, sire, are incurably romantic," began the Duke pompously. The King covered his ears with his hands and leaned on the balcony ledge. He tried to muffle the sound of his companion's irritating voice, but the Duke continued to rant about the impossibility of finding love in such a forced setting.

Meanwhile, the Prince was bowing to the Tremaine sisters, who were still clumsily curtsying and grinning, trying their best to spend as much time in front of the Prince as possible. When he lifted his head, he caught a glimpse of something magnificent. He perked up and walked between the two sisters, who thought he was showing interest in them. He briskly made his way to the balcony, where a striking young lady looked over the railing. The Prince went to her and took her hand. She turned around and their eyes locked. He bowed to her and she gracefully curtsied in return. The Prince took her other hand.

The Prince had fallen in love with none other than Cinderella!

It was love at first sight for both of them! And the King had been watching the whole encounter. He rubbed his eyes to make sure he wasn't dreaming. He rubbed his hands together with excitement. The whole time, the Grand Duke continued to blabber about love and fairy tales in the face of reality.

". . . a pretty plot for fairy tales, sire," chuckled the Duke. "But in real life, it was doomed to failure." He proudly grinned and cocked his head. He was quite pleased with himself.

But the King quickly returned the Grand Duke to reality.

"Failure, eh?" shouted the King. He grabbed the Duke's monocle and pulled it toward the Prince and Cinderella. He then shoved the Duke's head right into the monocle so he could see the excitement below them. "Ha!" laughed the King. "Take a look at that, you pompous windbag!"

Through the monocle they watched the Prince kiss Cinderella's hand. The Grand Duke was in awe.

The King continued to laugh with joy and anticipation. He summoned the orchestra to play a waltz, then whistled for the lights to be dimmed. He wanted the scene to be set just as he had imagined it. He was finally content.

"Well, now for a good night's sleep," said the King, yawning and stretching his arms. The Duke agreed. When the King headed for the exit, the Duke followed, but he was quickly halted.

"You will stay right here," the King said, pushing the Duke back into his chair. "See that they are not disturbed. And when the boy proposes, notify me immediately."

The King left through the curtains. The Duke was annoyed and frustrated. He had been made to look like a fool. He slumped disgustedly in the chair and mocked the King's request. But he was quickly startled by the King's voice. The King had stuck his head back through the curtains. If anything went wrong, he warned, the Duke would be held accountable.

With those words, the King glanced down at the lovely couple one last time. Then he officially made his exit from the balcony and danced down the hallway. He hummed and kicked up his heels. He even took a butler's hands and waltzed with him.

The King was very pleased. He disappeared into his room, shutting the huge doors behind him. His dreams that night would be sweet and satisfying.

Chapter 14

The Prince and Cinderella walked to the center of the dance floor hand in hand. At first, Cinderella was a bit intimidated by all the people watching them. But when the Prince put his hand on her hip and they stared deeply stared into each other's eyes, all her worries disappeared. Cinderella had come the ball to meet the Prince, but as soon as she had looked deeply into the eyes of this handsome gentleman, she had been smitten. She did not realize that young man she was dancing with *was* the Prince!

The couple waltzed around the floor with a soft light shining down on them. The crowd of guests encircled them. All eyes were on the Prince and his mysterious dance partner, who danced as if no one were watching.

The most curious onlookers of all were Lady Tremaine and her daughters. Anastasia and Drizella tried to sneak a peek over heads and under legs of the other guests.

"But who is she, Mother?" asked Anastasia curiously.

"Do we know her?" asked Drizella.

"Well, the Prince certainly seems to," replied Anastasia. "I know I've never seen her before."

"Nor I," replied Lady Tremaine as she peered over a gentleman's head for a closer look. The Prince and Cinderella danced closer to where the Tremaine women were standing. Though the Prince's body blocked Cinderella's face, Lady Tremaine did catch a glimpse of her.

"Wait," began Lady Tremaine, her eyes squinting. "There is something familiar about her." She walked quickly to catch up with the couple as they danced away from her.

Cinderella and the Prince waltzed off the dance floor and onto the balcony. Lady Tremaine followed them. Just as her view of the girl became clearer, a large red curtain with golden tassels closed in front of her. Her chance to identify the girl was thwarted.

The Grand Duke had pulled the curtain closed. He was following the King's orders. He wouldn't let anyone interrupt the Prince. He looked at Lady Tremaine and cleared his throat. That was his subtle way of telling her that she would not be allowed to proceed any further.

Chapter 15

Behind the curtain, the dancing continued. The Prince and Cinderella twirled around and stared deeply into each other's eyes. Their smiles stretched from ear to ear. They were both experiencing feelings they had never had before—it was true love.

They approached a small staircase leading to a lovely garden. They stopped dancing and the Prince took Cinderella's hand. They walked down the staircase without taking their eyes off each other. It was as if they were floating and nothing could bring them down to earth.

The couple strolled to a magnificent fountain.

The garden was dark. The only light came from the stars and their reflections on the water. Cinderella dipped her hand into the fountain and made the reflections twinkle even more. Once again, she and the Prince took each other's hands. They danced through shadows of columns and tall trees as the stars glittered in the sky.

With the moon shining down on them, they walked over a small bridge. Cinderella stopped and rested her hands on the railing, admiring the lovely river below. The Prince leaned on the same railing, admiring Cinderella. He was in awe of her beauty. He had never imagined that his night would end up this way. His heart was bursting with joy—and though he'd resisted his father's plan, the Prince had really fallen in love.

The lovestruck couple sat down on a bench. It was the perfect place for their first kiss. The Prince held Cinderella's arms and leaned in to kiss her. Cinderella's heart pounded in her chest.

Suddenly, the chime of a nearby clock tower sounded.

"Oh, my goodness!" cried Cinderella, looking at

the time on the clock. The first chime of midnight had struck!

"What's the matter?" asked the Prince.

"It's midnight!" replied Cinderella, standing up frantically.

"Yes, so it is," said the Prince, reaching out to her. "But why . . . ?"

Cinderella looked at the Prince and turned away. She knew she had to leave, and leave quickly.

"Goodbye," she said.

The Prince stood up and grabbed her arm.

"No, no, wait!" he began. "You can't go now!"

"Oh, I must!" Cinderella said. "Please, please, I must!"

"But why?" asked the Prince, confused and disappointed. He held on to her arms and did not want to let go.

Cinderella paused. She clearly couldn't tell this gentleman about her fairy godmother and the magic spell. She tried to think of another answer as she pulled away.

"The Prince," she replied. "I haven't met the Prince."

"The Prince?" he echoed. He dropped his hands to his side and raised his eyebrows. The Prince was now even more confused. Not only was the love of his life running away, she didn't even realize *he* was the Prince.

The clock chimed again.

"Goodbye!" yelled Cinderella. She ran up the staircase leading from the garden.

The Prince ran after her.

"No, wait! Come back," he said, reaching for her. "I don't even know your name! How will I find you?"

Cinderella hurried back into the ballroom through the closed drapes. The Grand Duke was asleep in a chair, keeping guard. One of the drapes hit him in the face as Cinderella burst through them, and he woke up. Cinderella waved goodbye to him. He smiled and sleepily waved back.

The clock chimed again.

The Duke then came to his senses and realized Cinderella was leaving.

"Young lady, WAIT!" yelled the Grand Duke, jumping out of his chair.

Just then, the Prince came running through the drapes after Cinderella.

"Wait!" he called to Cinderella. He started after her again, but a group of female guests swarmed him. They wanted their chance to talk to the Prince. He was cornered and unable to go after the girl he now loved.

Cinderella quickly made her way out of the ballroom and down the grand staircase. She was halfway down when she realized that one of her glass slippers had fallen off her foot. She stopped and turned around.

The clock chimed again.

Just as she was about to get the slipper, the Grand Duke came running after her. She turned back around without the slipper and hurried to her carriage.

"Mademoiselle!" called the Grand Duke. "Señorita, just a moment!" He picked up the glass slipper from the staircase and continued after her.

The clock chimed again.

Cinderella made it to the bottom of the steps. The carriage was waiting for her. The footman jumped up and down, motioning for her to hurry.

Cinderella climbed into the carriage and it quickly pulled away as the clock chimed again.

"Stop that coach!" called the Grand Duke. "Close those gates!"

But the coach sped through the gates right before they closed.

The clock chimed again.

The Grand Duke was frantic. He had been warned that he was responsible if anything went wrong. The King would be furious to find out that the potential mother of his grandchildren had gotten away—under the Duke's watch!

The Grand Duke called for the palace guard to go after the coach. A cavalry of men wearing black-and-red cloaks and helmets raced after Cinderella's coach on their horses. They followed it through the streets of town, over a bridge, and up and down hills.

The clock chimed again and again as the chase continued.

Chapter 16

Cinderella's magical coach was almost home—but something happened. The clock chimed for one last time. Midnight was struck! The coach slowed down. Its wheels turned back into long vines. It turned orange. The driver turned back into Cinderella's old horse. The four beautiful horses pulling the carriage turned back into mice. The footman became Bruno again.

In an instant, Cinderella found herself sitting on top of a pumpkin in her torn pink gown. Bruno and Major were by her side, and they were all stopped in the middle of the dirt road. The magic was gone. Everything changed back to the way it had been, just as the Fairy Godmother had said it would.

Suddenly, the sound of charging horses filled the air. Cinderella and the animals jumped up and ran into the bushes to get out of the way. The royal horsemen came speeding by and crushed the pumpkin in their path. They continued their chase for the coach holding the mystery girl from the ball. Unbeknownst to them, that girl was Cinderella, and she was kneeling on the roadside.

"I'm sorry," she said to Bruno and Major. "I guess I forgot about everything . . . even the time."

Major listened to Cinderella and smiled. His eyes opened wide. He wanted to hear more about her evening.

"But it was so wonderful!" continued Cinderella. Bruno smiled and wagged his tail. "And he was handsome!" Cinderella closed her eyes and clasped her hands. She was reliving the night in her head.

Gus and Jaq made their way to a large rock. Gus snuggled up to Jaq and closed his eyes. He, too, was imagining Cinderella's magical night.

Cinderella sighed and looked up to the stars.

"Oh, I'm sure even the Prince himself couldn't have been more . . ." She paused. Then she took a deep breath and stopped dreaming. Cinderella accepted that the ball was over. But that didn't matter. She was finally experiencing the happiness she had always hoped for—she had fallen deeply in love. Caught up in recalling every detail, she didn't realize that the man she had spent such a wonderful evening with was the guest of honor himself, the Prince!

Cinderella got to her feet, ready to move on. She heard a little voice from the ground. It was Jaq. He was jumping up and down, pointing to her feet. Cinderella looked down and saw that she still had on one glass slipper. She took it off her foot and held it close to her heart. The slipper sparkled, and its light illuminated Cinderella's face. She looked up to the stars once more. She wanted her fairy godmother to know how very grateful she was for such a magical evening.

"Thank you," she said, intending the words for her fairy godmother, wherever she was. "Thank you so much for everything."

Chapter 17

At the palace, the Grand Duke stood outside the King's bedroom door. He was preparing himself for his confrontation with the King. He had to break the news that the young lady disappeared. It wasn't going to be easy. He stood tall and proud and rehearsed his speech in front of an empty chair. He held the glass slipper in his hand. At last he was feeling confident, and he turned around, ready to knock on the door. But he quickly had a change of heart.

"No, I just can't," said the Grand Duke nervously. He slumped down and held his head in his hands. The King was going to be livid, and it was the Duke's fault. He looked through the keyhole in the door to procrastinate a little longer and to see what the King was doing. He wanted to see what the King's mood was like before telling him the bad news.

In the bedroom, the King was asleep on his gigantic bed. He wore a large white nightshirt and a purple nightcap. Between snores he let out a big chuckle. He was probably dreaming about playing with his adorable grandchildren, the Duke thought.

He finally found the courage to knock on the door, cutting the King's sweet dream short. The King awoke and collected himself.

"Come in!" he yelled.

The Duke opened the large door—slowly. He started to speak but was charged by the very excited King, who tackled him to the ground.

"So he's proposed already?" roared the King, leading the Duke into his room. "Tell me all about it. Who is she? Where does she live?" He slid a large chair under the Duke, forcing him to sit and reveal all the details.

The Duke tried to speak, but the King continued to rant.

“Eh, we’ve more important things to discuss,” he said. “Arrangements for the wedding, invitations, a national holiday, all that sort of thing!” He lit a cigar with his candelabra in celebration.

The Duke rose from his chair and tried to get a word in but was quickly quieted. The King pushed him back down into the chair and shoved a cigar into his mouth. The King’s excitement grew. Laughing, he shoved another dozen cigars into the Duke’s mouth and lit those with his candelabra, too.

“Bu-bu-but, sire, if you would only listen!” the Duke interrupted through the mouthful.

The King wouldn’t listen. He took out his large sword and pointed it at the Duke, who panicked and dropped to the floor, spitting out all the cigars but one.

“And for you, my friend,” the King said, aiming the sword at the Duke’s head. “A knighthood!”

The Duke knew he had to just come out and tell the King what had happened, no matter the consequences. He kneeled on the floor, quivering with fear.

“Sire, she got away!” he declared.

The short, stout King was too giddy with

excitement to hear at first. But when he realized what the Duke had said, his face turned as red as a beet with anger.

"She WHAT?" hollered the King, raising his fist in the air. "You traitor!" He was convinced that the Duke was working against him. He turned a deep shade of purple. His blood was boiling. He lifted his sword and it came crashing down inches from the Duke's nose, slicing the cigar in his mouth in half.

The Duke hid behind a chair, yelling for the King to stop. The King was infuriated and slashed at everything in his path.

"You were in league with the Prince all along!" yelled the King, chasing the Duke.

"I tried to stop her," replied the Duke. "Bu-bu-but she vanished into thin air!" He hid under a table, but the King came charging and sliced the table right down the middle.

"A likely story!" the King yelled.

The Duke jumped onto the King's bed and bounced high into the air.

"All we could find was this glass slipper," he said, holding it up to show the King.

The King bounced onto the bed. He went up and

the Duke went down. With each passing bounce, the King tried to strike him.

"The whole thing was a plot!" yelled the King, bouncing and waving his sword. He was still convinced that the Duke and the Prince had been working together to ruin the ball.

"But, sire, he loves her," the Duke protested. "He won't rest until he finds her. He's determined to marry her!"

"What? What did you say?" asked the King more gently. His demeanor changed and he actually cracked a smile.

The Duke bounced so high that he landed on the chandelier. His body draped over one of the chandelier's arms.

"The Prince, sire," he continued, "swears he'll marry none but girl who fits this slipper!" He presented the sparkling glass slipper to the King again.

The King bounced up to the chandelier and sat on another arm.

"He said that, did he?" asked the King, grabbing the slipper and kissing it happily. "Ha ha, we got it!" He laughed and sliced the wire holding the chandelier. With both men still on it, the chandelier crashed to the bed, making a hole straight through to the floor.

"But, sire," began the Duke, standing up in the mess. "This slipper may fit any number of girls."

"That's his problem," said the King, tossing the slipper back to the Duke. "He's given his word, and we'll hold him to it."

"No, no, Your Majesty, I'll have nothing to do with it," vowed the Duke. He turned his back to the King, put the slipper on the bed, and folded his arms in protest.

The King thrust his sword at the glass slipper and picked it up on the pointed tip. He slid the sword underneath the Duke's nose with the slipper dangling on the end.

"You'll try this on every maid in the kingdom!" ordered the King. "And if the shoe fits, bring her in."

The Duke trembled and looked at the sword under his nose.

"Ye-ye-yes, Your Majesty," he agreed.

By the King

A Proclamation

All loyal subjects of His Imperial Majesty are hereby notified by royal proclamation that in regard to a certain glass slipper, it is upon this day decreed that a quest be instituted throughout the length and breadth of our domain. The sole and express purpose of said quest is as follows to wit: that every maiden in our beloved kingdom shall try upon her foot this aforementioned slipper of glass, and should one be found whose foot shall properly fit said slipper, such maiden will be acclaimed the object of this search and the one and only true love of His Royal Highness, our noble Prince. And said Royal Highness will humbly request the hand of said maiden in marriage to rule with him over all the land as Royal Princess and future Queen.

Chapter 18

At the King's royal request, a formal proclamation was issued and posted outside the palace gates for all in the kingdom to see.

Word spread throughout the kingdom, and all the eligible maidens frantically prepared for the chance to try on the glass slipper. No one was as frantic as Lady Tremaine. Her daughters had another opportunity to become royalty, and she needed them dressed and ready. She would do anything in her power to have one of her daughters marry the Prince.

"Cinderella, Cinderella!" she shouted as she started up the stairs to her daughters' rooms. "Oh, where is that girl?"

Cinderella opened a door in the downstairs hallway with a broom in her hand.

"Yes, here I am," she responded politely.

"My daughters," Lady Tremaine asked abruptly. "Where are they?"

"I think they're still in bed," replied Cinderella.

"Well, don't just stand there!" yelled Lady Tremaine, glaring at Cinderella. "Bring up the breakfast trays at once—and hurry!" She feverishly picked up her skirt and continued up the stairs to Anastasia's and Drizella's rooms.

Cinderella stood in the open doorway and curiously watched Lady Tremaine hurry off. She wondered why her stepmother was in such a rush. But she obeyed, as usual, and went to fetch breakfast.

Gus and Jaq were standing in the doorway, too, and they were just as curious about Lady Tremaine's urgency.

"I wonder what's the matter with-a her," said Jaq, puzzled by all the excitement.

"Yes, what's the matter with her?" asked Gus, pointing up the stairs.

"I don't know. Let's find out!" said Jaq. He grabbed Gus's hand. They ran into an opening in the wall and scurried up to the next floor.

Lady Tremaine stormed into Drizella's room, calling her daughter's name. Drizella was still asleep in her bed, wearing a yellow nightgown and nightcap. Her bare feet stuck out from underneath the quilt. She was startled at the shrill sound of her mother's voice.

"What?" she said, stretching her arms and legs.

"Get up, quick, this instant!" Lady Tremaine opened the curtains and bright sunlight poured in. "We haven't a moment to lose!" Drizella squinted and covered her head with her quilt despite her mother's warning.

Lady Tremaine left Drizella's room and burst into Anastasia's. Gus and Jaq had made their way to Anastasia's room, too. They hid behind candles in the candelabra and listened to everything.

"Anastasia!" Lady Tremaine yelled. Anastasia was sound asleep and covered from head to toe with her quilt. Lady Tremaine went over to the bed and shook Anastasia to wake her. "Get up, Anastasia!"

Anastasia lifted her head from beneath her pillow and quilt. Her pink nightcap covered her eyes. "What's wrong?" she asked with a yawn.

Light filled the bedroom as Lady Tremaine opened the curtains. "Oh, everyone's talking about it . . . the whole kingdom," she growled. "Oh, hurry, he'll be here any minute!"

"Who will?" asked Drizella, who was standing in the doorway yawning and scratching her leg. She had finally dragged herself out of bed. Like Anastasia, she was still exhausted and couldn't understand her mother's insistence.

"The Grand Duke!" replied Lady Tremaine. "He's been hunting all night." She went to an armoire and sifted through clothes.

"Hunting?" asked Anastasia, even more confused.

"For *that* girl!" snarled Lady Tremaine.

Just then, Cinderella approached the door with a breakfast tray. She heard her stepmother ranting about the previous evening and her eyes widened with curiosity. She walked into the room so that she could hear more.

"The one who lost her slipper at the ball last night," continued Lady Tremaine. "They say he's madly in love with her."

Drizella sat down on Anastasia's bed.

"The Duke is?" asked Anastasia groggily, sleepily lifting her cap to reveal her eyes.

"No, no, no, the PRINCE!" shrieked Lady Tremaine.

Cinderella gasped and her eyes opened even wider.

"The Prince?" she whispered to herself. Cinderella finally realized that the man she had fallen madly in love with at the ball was the Prince himself. She dropped the tray and everything went crashing to the floor.

Lady Tremaine jumped and quickly turned toward Cinderella. She was disgusted with her. "You clumsy little fool!" she yelled. "Clean that up and then help my daughters dress."

Cinderella's stepsisters saw no reason to get up and dressed if the Prince was already in love with a girl. Drizella let out another big yawn and Anastasia rested her chin in her hand. Neither of them made any attempt to obey their mother. They both pulled Anastasia's quilt over their heads and chose to go back to sleep.

Lady Tremaine became even angrier. She ripped the covers off the girls and demanded their attention from the foot of the bed. "Now, you two listen to me," she insisted. "There is still a chance that one of you can get him."

Anastasia and Drizella peeked out of the quilt in unison. "One of us?" they asked.

Lady Tremaine changed her tone and became quiet and calculating. She leaned over the footboard. "Just listen," she said, waving her finger at her daughters. "No one, not even the Prince, knows who that girl is."

Gus and Jaq were still on stakeout in the candelabra. Gus popped his head out with excitement when he heard what Lady Tremaine had said.

"We know, we know!" he yelled. "Cinderelly, Cinderelly!" Jaq quickly quieted Gus. He pushed him back down under the candle in the candelabra. He didn't want to blow their cover.

"The glass slipper is their only clue," continued Lady Tremaine. "The Duke has been ordered to try it on every girl in the kingdom."

Cinderella was on the floor picking up the pieces from the dropped tray. She locked her eyes on her stepmother and listened intently to every word she said.

"And if one can be found whom the slipper fits," continued Lady Tremaine, "then by the King's command, that girl shall be the Prince's bride!"

"Bride?" Cinderella whispered. Her body froze. She couldn't believe what she had just heard.

Drizella and Anastasia couldn't believe it, either. They jumped off the bed and scrambled around the room to get ready. They wildly grabbed clothes and threw them at Cinderella. They commanded her to iron, mend, and sew.

Cinderella stood up holding the tray with a dreamy look on her face. She smiled from ear to ear and slowly batted her eyes. She paid no attention to the clothes being thrown at her. She was standing there, but her mind was somewhere else. She was in love and the Prince was in love with her—that was all she could think about.

After loading Cinderella down with even more clothes and making more requests, the stepsisters finally stopped. They noticed that she was not responding to them.

"What's the matter with her?" asked Anastasia, pointing to Cinderella.

"Wake up, stupid!" yelled Drizella.

"We've got to get dressed!" growled Anastasia.

Cinderella snapped out of her daydream and finally reacted to her stepsisters' demands, though she was still in a daze.

"Dressed?" said Cinderella, looking down at her own clothes. "Oh, yes, well, we must get dressed." She handed the pile of clothes back to Anastasia and turned away from her. She mumbled to herself about getting dressed as she walked out of the room.

Chapter 19

Anastasia and Drizella were shocked by Cinderella's actions. There were also furious and demanded that their mother do something. But Lady Tremaine once again shushed the girls. She curiously watched Cinderella walk down the hallway toward her room. Cinderella was humming a sweet song about love and swaying her arms from side to side. It was as if she were floating across the floor. She was happy, and Lady Tremaine needed to know why.

Lady Tremaine narrowed her cold emerald-green eyes and stared at the dancing Cinderella. *Could Cinderella be the girl from the ball? Is she the girl the Prince loves?*

Gus and Jaq had been watching Lady Tremaine, and they grew suspicious. Staying hidden, they followed her up the stairs, then perched on top of a beam. Lady Tremaine was heading for Cinderella's room, and she had a devious look on her face. The mice went to warn Cinderella.

Meanwhile, Cinderella was humming as she combed her hair in the mirror and twirled around. She was so happy. She couldn't wait for the Grand Duke to arrive with the glass slipper!

Suddenly, Gus and Jaq stormed into her room and climbed on top of her vanity. They jumped up and down on her hairbrush trying to get her attention. They called her name, but she continued to hum and look in the mirror. She finally noticed her little friends, but it was too late. At the same time, she saw her stepmother's reflection in the mirror. Cinderella gasped and turned toward Lady Tremaine just as she slammed Cinderella's door shut, then used her key to lock it. The only way the door could be opened again was with that key. Cinderella ran to the door and pulled on the handle, crying when it would not budge.

"Oh, you can't, you just can't," she pleaded. "You must let me out! You can't keep me in here! Oh, please!" Cinderella continued to pull on the door handle, trying to get out. She was sobbing. Poor Cinderella was devastated. Her wicked stepmother had once again crushed her chance for happiness. Cinderella knew that if the Grand Duke couldn't find her, then she couldn't try on the glass slipper and she'd never be with the Prince.

Lady Tremaine proudly tapped the key in her hand and then put it safely in her pocket. She walked back down the stairs feeling quite satisfied with her actions. Now there was no way Cinderella would have the opportunity to try on the glass slipper.

Gus and Jaq crawled underneath Cinderella's door and scowled at Lady Tremaine as she walked away. They were angry, and they knew they had to help Cinderella.

"We've gotta get that key, Gus-Gus," said Jaq excitedly. "We've just gotta get that key!"

Chapter 20

It had been a long day for the Grand Duke. He had traveled around the kingdom trying the glass slipper on every maiden. He was asleep in his coach as it approached his next stop. With each bump in the road, his head wobbled from side to side. He held a royal blue velvet pillow with gold trim and tassels on his lap. On the pillow was the glass slipper. A small purple blanket covered it for protection. But the blanket slid off of the pillow due to the bumpy ride.

The driver called for his horses to halt and the coach came to an abrupt stop. The footman sounded his horn, announcing the arrival of the Grand Duke. Startled, the Duke jumped from his seat and the pillow went flying off his lap, along with the glass slipper. But the sleepy man managed to catch the slipper in midair. He let out a huge sigh of relief and covered his face with one hand while he held the delicate slipper in the other. His daylong search had worn him down. He was exhausted, but by the King's orders, he had to continue. He was at his next stop—the Tremaine house.

Meanwhile, Gus and Jaq had run to the window when they heard the coach approach. The Grand Duke had arrived! The mice had to retrieve the key tucked away in Lady Tremaine's pocket, and they had to do it quickly. Once Cinderella got out of her room and put that slipper on, everyone would know the truth: she was the Prince's true love.

Anastasia and Drizella ran to a window. They were dressed in fancy gowns.

"Oh, Mother, he's here, he's here!" cried Anastasia.

"The Grand Duke!" cried Drizella.

Anastasia ran to the vanity for one final primping of her hair.

"Oh, I'm so excited, I just don't know what

else to do!" said Anastasia, fluffing her dress in the mirror.

Drizella came charging to the vanity for a final primping of her own and shoved Anastasia out of the way. She admired herself in the mirror and then powdered her nose. Anastasia came rushing back and jolted Drizella out of her way for her turn to powder.

"Girls!" warned Lady Tremaine. "Now, this is your last chance. Don't fail me." Holding a tall black cane, she walked to the front door with her head high. She opened the door to welcome their guests.

The Duke's royal assistant stood in the entryway and blew his brass horn. In his other hand he held the glass slipper atop the blue velvet pillow protected by the purple cover.

"Announcing His Imperial Grace the Grand Duke!" he declared. He then stepped aside.

The Grand Duke walked up the stairs wearing a tall blue hat with a red feather on top. He removed his hat upon entry and was greeted by Lady Tremaine.

"May I present my daughters, Drizella,

Anastasia," said Lady Tremaine pointing to each girl. The girls each curtsied and batted their eyelashes awkwardly.

"Your Grace," Anastasia greeted him. She smiled wide and stuck her finger under her chin to appear sweet and coy. But there was nothing sweet about her, and it was quite obvious to the Grand Duke.

"Oh, yes, charmed, I'm sure," replied the Grand Duke, cringing at the site of the unattractive sisters. He tried his best to maintain his composure.

The assistant then announced that the Grand Duke would read the royal proclamation. He uncurled the long scroll. The still-drowsy Duke began to read it out loud.

While the proclamation was being read, Gus and Jaq climbed up to the top of the coffee table. Lady Tremaine was standing near the table and the key was sticking out of her pocket. They wanted to get as close to her as possible. They needed to grab that key!

The Duke kept reading. When he came to the part about the glass slipper, the assistant lifted the cover off the plush pillow. He held it up with pride as the slipper sparkled on top. But the Duke's speech was interrupted.

"Why, that's my slipper!" shouted Drizella.

"It's *my* slipper!" yelled Anastasia.

The assistant was surprised by the girls' boldness. He tried to keep the slipper away from them.

Gus and Jaq were hiding in a teacup on the table. Gus got mad when he heard the sisters. "No, no, no! That's Cinderelly's slipper!" he yelled, climbing out of the teacup. Jaq pulled him back down. He covered Gus's mouth with his hat. They couldn't risk being discovered now, no matter how angry they were.

The stepsisters make a mad dash toward the assistant, trying to grab the glass slipper. He ducked and ran out from under them with the slipper intact. Then he hid behind the Grand Duke, away from the unruly girls.

"Girls, girls," said Lady Tremaine. "Your manners." She spoke to them calmly but glared at them with her most withering stare. "A thousand pardons, Your Grace," she said to the Grand Duke. "Please continue."

The Duke was quite annoyed by girls' behavior and the interruption, but he continued to read the proclamation.

Chapter 21

While the Grand Duke was reading the proclamation, Gus and Jaq made a plan. They quietly chatted in the cup and pointed to Lady Tremaine, who was listening to the Grand Duke intently. Jaq hopped out of the cup first and tiptoed over to Lady Tremaine. Her pocket was within reach and the key was visible. He leaned over the edge of the table. Gus held on to his tail and gently lowered him into the pocket. Jaq lifted the key. He tried to push it up so Gus could grab it, but Gus quickly waved his hands. Lady Tremaine was making a move toward the pocket! Scared, Gus ducked into the teacup and covered his eyes. He could barely watch.

Lady Tremaine glanced up the stairs at

Cinderella's door and stuck her hand in her pocket. She wanted to feel the key for reassurance. As long as she had that key, there was no way Cinderella was getting out of her room.

Jaq sweated profusely with fear as he tried to avoid being discovered. But once Lady Tremaine felt the key, she let go of it and then tapped the outside of her pocket. Jaq sighed with relief—but the mice were not out of trouble yet.

The Grand Duke finished reading the proclamation and relaxed, hoping this would be the last time that he had to read it. The assistant slid a chair under the Grand Duke, who plopped down to rest.

"You must be quite fatigued, Your Grace," said Lady Tremaine. She picked up the teapot and a cup—the cup Gus was hiding in! "May we offer you some tea?" she asked. Inside the cup, Gus frantically tried to avoid the hot tea about to hit his body.

"Thank you, madam, no," replied the Duke. Luckily for Gus, the tea never made it into the cup, and Lady Tremaine put the teapot and the cup back on the table. It was another close call for the little mice. "We must proceed with the fitting," continued the Duke.

"Of course," said Lady Tremaine, bowing to him. "Anastasia, dear!"

Anastasia sat in a chair and stuck out her foot. Only her toes were sticking out beneath her long, puffy dress. The assistant sat on a small stool in front of her and placed the glass slipper on her foot.

"There, I *knew* it was my slipper!" cheered Anastasia. The messenger clapped happily and lifted up her foot to show everyone in the room. But when he did, her dress slid down her leg, revealing her huge foot. The glass slipper didn't fit at all—it was only covering her toes! Almost her entire ugly foot was sticking out of the slipper.

"Oh, well, it may be a tad bit snug today . . . ," began Anastasia nervously. "You know how it is, dancing all night." She was embarrassed and twirled her hair nervously. She kept trying to make excuses as to why the slipper didn't fit. The assistant shrugged and rolled up his sleeves. He hopped on top of Anastasia's leg and tried pounding the slipper onto her foot, but it was no use. Anastasia became frustrated and began to yell at the assistant.

"It fit perfectly before. I don't think you're half trying," she said to him, lying. "Mother, can you—"

"Shhh, quiet, my dear," replied Lady Tremaine. "We mustn't disturb His Grace." Lady Tremaine pointed to the Grand Duke in the chair. He was asleep—and snoring! "Young man," she said to the assistant. "Are you sure you're trying it on the right foot?"

They were all so distracted by the fitting that no one had any idea what was going on in Lady Tremaine's pocket. Gus tied his tail to the spout of the teapot for leverage. Jaq pushed the key up and out of the pocket toward Gus. Gus grabbed hold of the key while Jaq dangled from the pocket, holding the other end of the key.

Lady Tremaine moved slightly and pulled the mice along with her. The teapot spout that Gus was tied to tipped as the mice were pulled in Lady Tremaine's direction. A hot drip of tea hit Gus's back. He jumped and his tail released from the spout. Gus went sliding down Lady Tremaine's dress, along with Jaq and the key. They spun across the floor. Gus hit the wall with the key wedged up against him, but Jaq got up and quickly pulled Gus to his feet.

"Upstairs!" whispered Jaq, pointing. It would be a long climb to Cinderella's room, but they had to do it. The mice lifted the heavy key up each steep step. It was so hard for them! They tried to move as quickly as possible. Beads of sweat dripped down Gus's tiny head as he worked feverishly to keep up with Jaq.

Meanwhile, Anastasia was still yelling at the assistant to get the slipper to fit.

"Why can't you hold still a minute!" she screamed, kicking the assistant with her big foot. The assistant slammed into the piano and banged against the keys, waking the Grand Duke. The Grand Duke was shocked by all the commotion.

"Oh, my word!" he said angrily. "Enough of this! The next young lady, *please*!"

Chapter 22

Gus and Jaq finally made it to the top of the first staircase. They were now in the hallway to Lady Tremaine's and the sisters' bedrooms. Poor little Gus could hardly walk. He was so tired. But Jaq was on a mission, and he moved even more quickly than before. He had to get Cinderella out of her room before the Grand Duke left! Jaq and Gus crawled under the door to the next floor and slid the key along with them.

Gus looked up and saw another great big staircase. Cinderella slept high in the attic tower, and the mice had a long way to go. Gus pointed and shook his head. He didn't think he could go any farther. He fainted at the mere sight of all the stairs. Jaq lifted him up and pulled on his hair to open his eyes, then slapped his chin to wake him and patted his back for encouragement. Gus snapped out of it and regained some strength. Still dragging the key, the mice continued up the steps one by one.

Meanwhile, Cinderella was crying in her room. She was leaning against the door when she heard little voices. She looked through the keyhole and saw Gus and Jaq coming up the stairs.

"We're coming, Cinderelly!" said Jaq to himself to as he pulled the key up the last step. Gus and Jaq finally made it to the top. They pushed the key toward Cinderella's door.

Jaq slid under the door first. Gus was right behind him, pushing the key.

"You got the key!" said Cinderella excitedly. "How did you ever manage . . . ?"

Suddenly, there was a dark shadow over Gus. Then came a big crash. Cinderella gasped. It was Lucifer! He had slammed a giant bowl down on top of Gus—and Gus had the key!

"Lucifer!" yelled Cinderella. "Let him go! Please let him go!" Through the keyhole, she saw Lucifer holding the bowl over Gus. She begged the cat to release her friend. The other mice watched from holes in the wall. They wanted to help but didn't know how.

Jaq slid back under the door to confront Lucifer. Jaq was mad! He rolled up his sleeves and yelled, "Let him go! Let him out!" He ran toward Lucifer and grabbed on to his swinging tail. Lucifer swung his tail ferociously, but Jaq managed to hang on. He spread the fur on a piece of Lucifer's tail and bit him—hard!

Lucifer screeched in pain and jumped into the air, leaving the bowl on the ground. Jaq tried to move the bowl before Lucifer landed, but he wasn't quick enough. Lucifer landed on the floor, causing the bowl to bounce in the air—and release Gus! Gus tried to run with the key, but the bowl landed right back on top of him! Lucifer jumped onto the bowl and held it between his paws. The mean old cat smirked as he clutched his prize.

The other mice couldn't sit back and watch from the walls anymore. A couple of them grabbed forks that were hidden in the walls and charged Lucifer. It was no use. Lucifer hit the ends of the forks with his paw and flipped the mice into the air, smashing them against the wall.

A few other mice lit a candle and rolled it toward Lucifer on a spindle. Lucifer turned around and took a deep breath. He blew out the flame inches from his face. He laughed proudly.

Suddenly, Lucifer was hit on the head from above. Two birds had dropped plates and a pot on him. The plates broke as they crashed to the floor. Lucifer leaped up, trying to claw at the birds. But the birds kept dropping plates on his head.

Once again, Gus had a chance to escape. The bowl bounced off him in all the commotion. He looked around and saw that the coast was clear. He started to run away but realized he'd forgotten the key. He turned back to get it, but before he could escape, Lucifer smashed the bowl on top of him again.

In her room, Cinderella listened to the ruckus outside her door. She had an idea. "Quick, get Bruno!" she shouted through the keyhole.

Two little birds heard Cinderella's request and went flying out the window to get Bruno in the barnyard. Bruno was asleep on the ground outside the stable. The birds hovered over him, chirping as loudly as they could. They were trying to tell him that Cinderella needed his help. Bruno didn't budge. They tugged on his long, floppy ears and he just rolled his eyes. The horse in the stable knew something was wrong. He let out a huge whinny. It scared Bruno and he jumped up. Then he finally paid attention to the chirping birds. He followed them toward the house, running as fast as he could.

Chapter 23

In the parlor, the fitting continued. Drizella screamed at the assistant as he tried to squeeze the slipper onto her foot.

"I'll do it myself!" she yelled. "Get away from me. I'll make it fit." She hit him on the head with her own shoe and kicked him away. He fell to the ground in a daze. She took the slipper and shoved it onto her foot. Her foot was nearly bent in half, but she managed to squeeze into the tiny glass slipper.

"There!" she said, holding up her foot crammed into the shoe.

"It fits!" declared Lady Tremaine with her eyes open wide.

"It fits?" echoed the Grand Duke, standing up from his chair for a closer look.

Everyone stared at Drizella's foot. Within seconds, her big foot popped out of the tiny slipper and the slipper went flying into the air.

The Duke gasped. He and his assistant jumped and ran to catch the slipper before it crashed to the ground. They didn't see each other and collided. The Duke fell on top of the assistant, stretched out his arm, and caught the glass slipper on one finger. He let out a huge sigh of relief.

"Oh, Your Grace, I'm dreadfully sorry," said Lady Tremaine. "It shan't happen again."

"Precisely, madam!" replied the Duke angrily.

Bruno made his way into the house and ran toward Cinderella's room. When he reached the top of the stairs to the attic, he saw Lucifer hovering over a bowl. He growled angrily and Lucifer hissed and screeched in fear.

All the cat's hairs stood up on his body. He backed up against Cinderella's door, clawing and hissing. He abandoned the bowl with Gus underneath.

Bruno lunged toward the cat and Lucifer jumped on top of the window ledge to get away. Bruno leaped up to reach the ledge, trying to bite him. Lucifer had no place to go but down. He jumped out the window to get away from the angry dog.

Jaq and three other mice ran over to the bowl and lifted it off Gus. Gus held the key tightly with his eyes closed. Jaq tried to pull Gus off the key, but Gus just wouldn't budge. He held on with all his might. Jaq tapped on his head and called his name. Gus shook his head no with his eyes still shut.

Jaq tugged on his tail so hard that he finally let go of the key. He opened his eyes and smiled. He was so glad to see Jaq and not Lucifer. Jaq picked up the heavy key and Gus helped him slide it under Cinderella's door.

Chapter 24

The Grand Duke was ready to leave. He stood in the doorway of the house with one final question.

"You are the only ladies of the household . . . I hope . . . I presume?" he asked.

"There's no one else, Your Grace," replied Lady Tremaine confidently.

"Quite so," he said. "Good day!" He put his hat on, turned away, and headed down the outside stairs.

Suddenly, there was the sound of a young lady's voice. She was on the landing at the top of the inside staircase.

"Your Grace!" the girl called. It was Cinderella! "Please wait! May I try it on?"

Lady Tremaine, Anastasia, and Drizella looked up at Cinderella in shock—their jaws had dropped and their eyes were wide. How had she ever managed to escape?

The Duke turned back around and smiled. He removed his hat and looked through his monocle. He saw a beautiful young girl running down the stairs. He happily walked back into the house.

"Pay no attention to her," said Lady Tremaine.

"It's only Cinderella, our scullery maid," said one sister.

"It's ridiculous, it's impossible, she's out of her mind!" yelled the other sister.

"Yes, yes, just an imaginative child," said Lady Tremaine. She walked toward the Duke with her back to the stairway. She tried to block Cinderella's path and stop the Duke from getting any closer to her. But she couldn't.

"Madam," began the Duke. "My orders were every maiden." He continued toward Cinderella, moving Lady Tremaine to the side. His smile was warm. Lady Tremaine's eyes were cold with fear.

The Grand Duke walked over to the bottom

step and took Cinderella by the hand. "Come, my child," he said, guiding her to a chair.

The Grand Duke then waved for his assistant, who excitedly stood in the doorway. He held the plush purple pillow with the glass slipper on top. He nodded and ran toward Cinderella happily.

Lady Tremaine had her eyes on Cinderella and the Duke, and then on the assistant and the glass slipper. She had to think fast. The wicked stepmother smiled deviously. Lightning quick, she stuck out her cane and tripped the assistant. He fell flat on his face, still holding the pillow with the slipper on it. When the pillow hit the ground, the glass slipper went flying into the air. It hit the floor right at the feet of Cinderella and the Duke—and shattered into a million pieces.

The Duke was devastated. He kneeled down, trying to pick up the shards. He had to put the pieces back together—he had to fix that glass slipper!

"Oh, no!" he yelled. He slid to the floor, banging his hands on his head. "Oh, no, this is terrible!" Then his mood changed. He became quite nervous. "The King! What will he say?"

Lady Tremaine smiled smugly. She was proud of herself. Cinderella would never have the chance to try on the glass slipper, and she would never find happiness.

The Duke was still panicking. He sat on his knees and thought about the King's reaction. "What will he do?" asked the Duke, grabbing his throat.

"Perhaps . . . this would help," said Cinderella, reaching into her pocket.

"No, no, nothing can help now," cried the Duke, still sifting through the broken glass. "Nothing!"

"But, you see, I have the other slipper!" said Cinderella. She held the glass slipper up in the air.

Lady Tremaine gasped.

The Duke grinned from ear to ear. His fingers shook with excitement. He took the slipper from Cinderella and kissed it repeatedly. He held it up in the air and watched it sparkle.

Jaq, Gus, and the other mice and birds had seen everything from the landing of the staircase. They jumped with joy, dancing and cheering.

The Grand Duke delicately placed the glass slipper on Cinderella's foot.

It didn't just fit—it fit perfectly, and it sparkled more brightly than ever before.

Chapter 25

Wedding bells rang throughout the kingdom. The sun was shining. White doves circled the large clock tower. It was noon, and Cinderella and the Prince had just been married.

They exited the church happily as husband and wife. The King's royal guard stood at attention as they watched the couple run down the red-carpet-lined staircase.

Cinderella was a beautiful bride. Her white gown floated down the long staircase. Two bluebirds held the ends of her long, lacey veil. The handsome groom held his bride's hand proudly. It was the greatest day of their lives.

It was also the greatest day of the King's life.

He and the Grand Duke stood at the top of the stairs throwing rice at the newlyweds. They smiled and waved as they watched the couple take their first steps as husband and wife.

Halfway down the stairs, Cinderella stopped running. The Prince stopped and looked up at his bride. Cinderella realized she lost her shoe. She looked back and saw it a few steps behind them. It had slipped off her foot just like the glass slipper on the night she'd met the Prince—but this time, she went back to get it. When she bent down to pick it up, she was met by her father-in-law, the King. He kneeled down, picked up the shoe, and placed it on her foot. She kissed the top of his head and ran back down the stairs with her Prince. The King sat on the step and grinned from ear to ear. He blushed as he waved goodbye to the beautiful couple.

At the bottom of the stairs, the Prince helped Cinderella climb into their wedding carriage. Then he climbed in after her. The wedding guests continued to throw rice and confetti. Cinderella and the Prince waved goodbye to the onlookers as the carriage pulled away.

Gus, Jaq, and a couple of the other mice stood on top of the church's ledge. They were dressed in long blue-and-gold coats. Their hats were blue with tall purple feathers. They looked like royalty themselves. They, too, threw rice at the carriage and jumped up and down happily.

Major, Cinderella's trusty old horse, led the wedding carriage, and her beloved dog, Bruno, ran along its side.

Cinderella waved goodbye to her dear mice friends as the carriage pulled away. They all waved back to their wonderful and deserving friend.

Cinderella's dreams of happiness had come true. She had never stopped hoping. The young girl who had tended to her family's every need was finally free. She was no longer anyone's servant—she was a princess! Most importantly, Cinderella was in love and was loved in return.

Cinderella and the Prince shared a kiss as their wedding carriage rolled off down the road.

And they lived happily ever after!

THE END